Dedicated to Dave,
Josh and Adam
for all their
love and support

It was the start of another busy day in Chakra Town.

The sun was rising, tinging the houses with a beautiful red glow and all the Mental Health monsters were getting ready to go about their business – all that is, except Bixbite.

Normally Bixbite was full of energy, full of life and extremely healthy, but today he had woken up feeling very off-colour. Instead of sporting his usual bright red fur coat that helped him feel extremely safe, today his fur was limp and lifeless and PINK!

"Oh no!" he thought. "What's wrong with me?"

And then he remembered.......

Today was the day he was supposed to start in a new class at a school and he was scared – very scared.

"What if I don't fit in?" he thought.

"What if I can't do the work?"

"What if people don't like me?"

He just couldn't stop his brain from whirring with all the bad thoughts. And the more he thought about them, the more stressed, anxious and worried he became. And the more stressed, anxious and worried he was, the pinker he became.

"Morning Bixbite," said his mum enthusiastically, as he crept downstairs for breakfast.

"What a beautiful morning and what an exciting day you have ahead."

"I DO NOT HAVE AN EXCITING DAY AHEAD!" shouted Bixbite, "AND IT ISN'T A BEAUTIFUL MORNING, IT IS A TERRIBLE MORNING!"

"Oh!" said his mum, taken aback - and then she noticed his colour.

"Oh, Bixbite," she cried, "you are pink. This won't do at all!"

And she walked over to him and gave him a great big hug.

"Are you feeling scared?"

"Are you feeling stressed?"

"Are you worried that you won't know what to do?"

"Yes," mumbled Bixbite quietly, "and all my energy seems to have just disappeared. What if I can't do anything mum? What if everything is too hard?"

"Well," said his mum, "sometimes things will seem hard, sometimes things will seem scary and stressful. If you think too much about these feelings, you will start to feel insecure that you won't be able to cope. And that is when your energy dips."

"What we need to do, is get you thinking more positively and start boosting your energy, and I know just the thing to start with."

"Really!" exclaimed Bixbite. "Will it make me red again?"

"Absolutely," laughed his mum, "and once you learn all these techniques you will be able to use them whenever you feel stressed and worried again. And the best bit –"

"What, what?" said Bixbite.

"The more you practise what I'm going to tell you, the stronger and more confident you will feel. And the more confident you feel, the easier things become, and the better you will feel."

"Let's get to it then," enthused Bixbite.

"OK," laughed his mum. "The first thing to remember is that, when you feel stressed or worried, scared or insecure, your red energy dips, which in turn makes your red fur colour fade.

Because we are red monsters, these feelings affect all of us and that is why you have gone pink (your red colour has gone paler)".

"Ah!" exclaimed Bixbite.

"But in humans, red energy is found at the bottom of their spine. When they have the feelings you have had, it affects their energy and their feelings of safety and security too."

"So come on, what do I have to do?" asked Bixbite impatiently.

"OK, OK," grinned his mum. "First, let's feed you up with red foods because these will help to get some red colour and energy back inside of you."

"Ooh, strawberries and cherries please," said Bixbite.

And as soon as his mum had prepared a bowl of delicious red fruit, Bixbite had eaten them.

"Yu...." he sighed. And then he stopped.

"My fur! Mum, look at my fur. My feet are starting to turn red again!"

"What did I say?" said his mum. "Now for the next trick."

"Go and get your red school bag and your red pencil case and your red pencil – anything that you need for school that is red."

And off Bixbite rushed, coming back a few minutes later with everything his mum said.

And guess what?

His arms had started to go red again.

"Wow!" said Bixbite. "This is amazing. So if I start to feel worried, scared, stressed or unsafe or I can feel my energy dropping, I can just eat red foods and surround myself with anything red?"

"Yep," said his mum, "and humans often wear red as well, but that's not all..."

"No?" queried Bixbite.

"No," said his mum. "The red energy centre is energized by earth and nature, so if you go outside in your bare feet and stamp and march on the ground it will help get rid of any bad energies associated with all those feelings you had, and instead fill you up with good energy."

"Ooh, this sounds fun," said Bixbite, and he rushed outside and started to march and stamp.

As he did so, his tummy started to turn red.

"If you want to do it while banging a drum or listening to drumming music that will be even better!" shouted his mum through the window, as she turned on the radio.

"Does the music need to have certain notes in it?" said Bixbite, as he continued to march around.

"Well the key of C is good for the red energy centre," explained his mum, "and it just so happens I have a song that fits and you might want to learn as it will help you through the day."

"Cool!" said Bixbite. "This is soooooooo good. Please teach me the song mum! Then I can go outside and marchy and stamp around and sing the song.

And so his mum taught him the song.

After a few goes with the song, Bixbite looked at himself in the mirror and saw that his tummy had turned red but there were still a few patches of pink left in his fur.

"Mum," he moaned, "I'm still not totally back to normal."

"Don't panic," his mum laughed. "There are three more things I want to tell you about and then you'll be ready to start school full of energy and confidence.

So the first one is to find some pictures of all the things that make you happy and all the things that make you feel safe and try to do at least one of those things or surround yourself with one of those things every day, even if it is just for 5 minutes.

Then maybe next week we can start to put them together in something known as a vision board."

"OK, so I love drawing and reading," said Bixbite. "and I feel safe at home and with my friends – is that what you mean?"

"Exactly," laughed his mum, "but I'm sure you can think of more.

For now though, the second thing I want you to try and do is notice when you are having thoughts that make you feel sad, that make your heart beat faster or make you breathe faster.

When you do, use some affirmation cards to help you think happier thoughts or make you more confident.

You could even use the cards as a bookmark so you can put them in your book and look at them all the time."

"Oh mum, you are amazing. Thank you!" exclaimed Bixbite.

"You are welcome, Bixbite. There is just one more thing I want you to do, which I think will get all your colour back. And that - is a meditation."

"A medi – what?" said Bixbite intrigued.

"A meditation," said his mum. "It is when you spend some time relaxing and using your imagination to think of positive things."

"Ah!" said Bixbite. "It sounds intriguing. Can we do it now? I really want to be red all over before I go to school. I am feeling so much more confident and so much more energetic already and I know what to do if I start to feel stressed and worried. I just need to be fully red now."

"Well, this will do it," said his mum. "Are you ready?"

"You bet," said Bixbite, and together they did the meditation.

And do you know what?

At the end of the meditation Bixbite was totally red again.

"Yay!" he exclaimed. "I know I can do anything now. I am even ready for school. It's going to be awesome."

And as he left his mum smiling, he set of with a spring in his step, excited to see what the day had in store for him.

Here is the meditation that Bixbite did with his mum.
Why don't you have a go?

Just lie down on the floor, get yourself comfortable and close your eyes.

Place one hand on your tummy and take a deep breath in so you can feel your hand rising up with your tummy.

And breathe out feeling your hand go back down.

And in – feel your hand rise.

And out – feel your hand fall.

Now this time as you take a breath in, imagine that you are breathing in a special superpower that allows you to float above the ground and as you go back to breathing normally just imagine yourself rising higher and higher into the sky until you reach a beautiful rainbow.

See yourself floating down until you land in the red part of the rainbow and notice how that red colour completely surrounds you and makes you feel totally safe.

As you sit there you notice that it has started to rain but that the raindrops aren't just ordinary raindrops they are magic raindrops.

Put your hand out to catch one and see that it has a little door in it just waiting for you to put in a feeling or a problem that you don't want any more.

In that raindrop I want you to pop in anything that makes you feel angry, anything at all – and once you have done this close the door and let the raindrop go.

See it as it disappears out of sight.

Now I want you to catch another raindrop and in this raindrop pop in anything that makes you feel stressed, anything at all and again let the raindrop go.

Then catch another raindrop and put in anything that worries you and let it go.

And finally catch one more raindrop and pop in anything you feel scared about – maybe not wanting to try new things, maybe thinking you are not good enough or that you don't fit in at school or at a club.

Put it all in and let that raindrop go.

Now as the raindrops disappear from sight you see some fairies and elves dressed in beautiful red gowns and suits, floating up towards you and each one of them is carrying an envelope.

As the first of these magical people flies over your head, you can see on the envelope are the words, "I am safe" and as you watch, see how they take out some magic dust and sprinkle it over your head.

Then the next magical person flies over your head and on their envelope are the words, "I am confident". Once again they sprinkle their magic dust over you.

Then a third magical person flies over with their envelope that says, "I am strong and healthy" and they sprinkle their magic dust over you.

And finally a fourth magical person flies over your head with an envelope which says, "I love me" and sprinkles all their magic dust over you.

Then just as quickly as they arrived, they disappear but you notice that you are now surrounded by the most amazing bubble of beautiful white light that fills you with confidence, positivity, energy and love.

And as you sit there in your special bubble feeling better than you have for ages you see a vast slide appear going from the rainbow all the way back down to earth and with another deep breath you step onto it and zoom all the way down and back into this room.

And as you become aware of the room you are in now, know that you are safe and secure and have everything inside of you to help you to be absolutely awesome.

So now just take a deep breath in and out and open your eyes ready to carry on with your amazing day.

Here is the song Bixbite
learnt with his mum

I am safe, I'm secure. I am loved
I am safe, I'm secure. I am loved
Whenever I feel scared, whenever I feel mad
I surround myself in red and stamp my feet instead

Activities that will help to open your red energy centre whenever you feel unsafe, insecure, worried or scared

- Think of and try to eat as many red foods as you can.

- Find as many red things as you can around your house and keep them close

- Spend some time marching and stamping around (barefoot and outside if possible)

- Find some pictures of all the things that make you happy and all the things that make you feel safe and put them in a scrap book so you can look at them often

KIND
TALENTED I AM... STRONG
BRAVE DESERVING
UNIQUE

More activities that will help to open your red energy centre whenever you feel unsafe, insecure, worried or scared

- Practice saying these affirmations every day

I AM SAFE AND SECURE

I AM AMAZING

Why not write them on paper, laminate them and put them around the house or use them as a bookmark and every time you see one, say it to yourself

TALENTED KIND STRONG
BRAVE I AM... DESERVING
UNIQUE

Printed in Great Britain
by Amazon